FLUNKING

M̶ _ _ _ _

#630

$7 99

By L. Lee Shaw

ILLUSTRATIONS BY LINDA BREWSTER

Boho
Books

Molalla, Oregon

This is a work of fiction. Names, characters, places, and incidents are either products of the author's imagination or, if real, are used fictitiously.

Flunking Magic

Copyright © 2018 by L. Lee Shaw

ISBN: 978-0-9907073-0-1 (paperback)

Printed in the United States of America

Boho Books paperback edition/September 2018

DEDICATION

To kids everywhere who are sure they are all wrong!

CHAPTER 1

When ReeCee Toadmite was born, it caused quite a stir in Williwog Woods. The daughter of a witch and a warlock is expected to come into the world with a head full of black hair, dark eyes, and green skin. ReeCee wasn't even close.

Witch looks weren't the only thing ReeCee lacked. Her magic kinda stunk as well. Actually, her magic was such a muddled mess she had ended up being placed in the special education class at school this year.

But today was the first Saturday of October, and Saturday was ReeCee's day to do something she dearly loved . . . clean her room.

Humming to herself, she was busy washing cobwebs in her little cauldron. The displaced web owners were all lined up on the windowsill glaring at her, and many little spider toes were tapping impatiently.

Carefully shaking the webs dry, she didn't notice the bat fluttering in through her open bedroom window.

"You know, you are probably the only kid in the whole of Williwog Woods who cleans their room. I am pretty sure that's not normal," the bat said as it hovered watching her.

"Hi, Digby," ReeCee answered. She began rehanging the webs under the supervision of her pet spider, Geoffrey, who was swinging from a button on her black dress.

"You better not have starched them again. Last time you did, the spiders were bouncing everywhere like Ping-Pong balls when they tried to jump on a fly," Digby said.

The bat transformed into a boy about ReeCee's age. He held out a small bag. "Mom sent some bloodworms for Geoffrey. She thought they might make him feel better."

ReeCee carefully lifted the spider in her hand as she unhooked his silken strand from her button. Geoffrey slowly limped off onto her bed.

"Are they feeling any better?" Digby asked.

Geoffrey answered by standing and holding up four legs with bandaged ankles,before falling over on his back. He waved all eight legs in the air for a moment, then curled them in towards his abdomen, pretending to be dead.

"Come on, Geoffrey," ReeCee said. "Dr. Octobury said they were just mild sprains and would be better in a few days."

Geoffrey didn't move.

ReeCee blew out her breath crossly as she began picking up the other spiders and returning them to their webs. By the time she had everyone home, Geoffrey had righted himself and was munching on the bloodworms.

"Wanna help?" she asked, handing a box to Digby.

"Do what?"

"Oliver asked if he could have all the dust bunnies I find under my bed. He's collecting them for some kind of Halloween project."

ReeCee wriggled under her bed and began handing Digby the weird little creatures composed mostly of air, dust, and fuzzels when Beatrice darted into the room, loudly chittering.

"What's she saying?" ReeCee asked in a muffled voice.

Digby listened as the little bat circled his head. "She's saying 'something wicked this way comes.'"

Almost immediately, they heard footsteps in the hall. ReeCee's cousin Edweena, who was twelve and one-quarter years old, sashayed in through the door.

"Hey, ReeCee, Mom wants to know if you want to come to Mausoleum Mall with us. I wanna look for something really ravin' to wear for the Dragon in the Dungeon dance."

She stopped when she realized she was talking to ReeCee's feet. "You know, cleaning your room is just totally maggoty dumb. If you don't quit it by the time you're my age, you aren't going find a boyfriend as cool as Beau."

"You're only two years older than me," ReeCee said as she squeezed back out from under her bed.

"Besides, I don't think Beau is really your boyfriend." Digby said. "I think he's got a thing for Hatshepsut Mummbum. I heard him

3

telling Larry Luppo that Hattie's linen wrappings were getting real interesting."

"Right. A rodent like you is friends with Beau Chomp," Edweena said, flipping her hair back over her shoulder.

"No, but I was standing in the lunch line right behind him and Larry while they were staring. Their tongues were hanging halfway to their knees and they were licking their chops. It was pretty disgusting, actually," Digby replied.

Edweena rolled her eyes. "Yeah, I so totally believe that Beau's checking out someone who has been undead for eons."

"You know, a lot of Williwog is undead, and maybe some parts of Hattie are getting undeader than others."

Edweena answered by plopping on the floor and pulling her eyeFone out of her bag. She punched the icon that brought up the hourly Fairest of All rankings and began scrolling through them.

Looking over her shoulder, Digby chanted "Mirror, mirror on the wall, will Edweena ever make the list at all?"

With an angry snort, Edweena jumped to her feet. "You guys are such losers. I am so not going anywhere with you." She headed to the door where she paused, flipped her black hair again, and said "Seventeen and a half inches," before flouncing out.

Digby looked at ReeCee. "And that means what?" he asked.

"That's how long her hair is now. She measures it every day."

Digby shrugged, "So?"

"So witches are supposed to have long, scraggly hair. It really does look pretty cool streaming out all horrid and tangled when riding a broom in the light of the great harvest moon."

Digby shrugged again. "And why does Edweena think you care about her hair?"

"Because I don't have witch hair. It won't grow long. It's light brown, and I can't get it to tangle, no matter how hard I try. Geoffrey

can't ride in it. He just falls, kerplop, in a heap on the floor. That's how he sprained his ankles," ReeCee said sadly. "I was going to wear him for Creepy-Crawly Day at school, but he slid out when we were deciding where he would look best."

"Well, I think your hair is just fine. It goes good with your blue eyes."

Digby paused.

ReeCee was scrunching her face up, which made her nose twitch.

"What are you doing?"

"I'm practicing scary witch squints," ReeCee said.

"Oh."

She stopped. "They're not scary, are they?" she asked.

Digby shook his head. "Not scary."

"Edweena's are scary. Really scary."

"ReeCee, Edweena is really scary without squinting. Why would you want to be like her, anyway?"

"I don't, but she can do real witch stuff. If I don't learn to do real witch stuff, Mrs. Murgatroyd is going to turn me into a toadstool right after she flunks me."

"Gargoyle. I'm pretty sure Mrs. M. always turns kids who flunk into gargoyles."

CHAPTER 2

The following Monday morning, ReeCee headed out the door of her house carrying a box and bumping her broom down the stairs behind her.

Her broom was actually pretty awesome. It was custom painted with sparkly witch symbols and tricked out with lots of cool features. But, no matter how much she tried though, she could not make that broom—or any broom—fly.

This was super-embarrassing. Riding a broom was another of those things that is pretty much expected of real witches. It was doubly super-embarrassing for ReeCee because her father owned the biggest broom store in Williwog Woods.

School brooms filled with littles who were too young to motate to school on their own flew by as she crossed the street to Digby's house.

Leaning her broom against the front door frame, she lightly tapped the entry code on the door panels. It creaked open.

Inside, she called softly, "Digby?"

Although Mrs. Noktern had reassured her many times that the family slept like the dead during the day, ReeCee still worried about disturbing them.

When she didn't get a response, she peeked around the corner into the Noktern's family room.

Across the room, a small light still shone on papers spread across Digby's art table and piled on the floor around his chair. ReeCee guessed he had probably stayed up too late working on drawings for his comic book since the coffin lying in the window seat was still closed.

She tiptoed to the coffin and knocked on the lid. "Hey, Digby, get up. We're gonna be late for school."

The lid slowly lifted, revealing a soft glow. A bat was snuggled under the collar of a pale blue pajama top. It stretched its wings and yawned before flapping sleepily out and up the stairs.

While she waited, ReeCee watched as, one by one, the night lightning bugs encircling the inside of the coffin turned off their butt lights and fluttered down to Digby's pillow. There they pawed it before making three precise turns and lying down with their wings spread over them like tiny blankets.

Almost immediately, Digby was back at her side, fully dressed, and drinking something dark red from a glass.

"Ewww, don't drink blood in front of me. You know I think it's gross."

"It's just beet juice with bilberry. Mom thinks if I could see better in the dark I'll quit being scared of it. What's in the box?"

"The dust bunnies we collected for Oliver on Saturday. Ready?"

Digby fastened on his cape before slinging his book bag over one shoulder. The door closed itself when the two kids stepped outside.

As they turned in the direction of school, they heard a familiar voice above them.

"Hey, specks, didn't anybody tell you real witches ride their brooms to school? Oh, wait, my bad. No real witches here. Sorry!"

Edweena and her two sidekicks, Zink and Pym, cackled loudly as they flew by.

ReeCee hated it when other kids called her a "speck" just because she was in special ed. It made her want to slap an ugly on them, but her mom was always telling her to ignore them. However, since it was coming from her cousin, ReeCee yelled after them, "Digby's not a speck!"

Beside her, Digby cleared his throat. "Actually, I'm pretty sure I am a speck. Or kinda one."

"You're not in special education. You take regular classes."

"ReeCee, I am the only vampire kid in Williwog Woods who goes to school during the DAY. Every other vampire kid goes to night school."

ReeCee tilted her head as she considered that for a moment. "But you're not assigned to the Room of Doom."

"That's because I can do all the vampire stuff, I'm just too scared to do it in the dark."

"At least you know how to vampire. My magic is so horrible, my spells never do what they're supposed to. I dunno, sometimes I think Edweena is right. Maybe I'm not really a witch at all."

"Are you kidding? Your spell last week was great!"

"They were supposed to be flies, Digby. I didn't get flies. And today, we're supposed to do the whole prince-into-frog thing. If I can't even cast a simple fly spell and get flies, I don't know how I'm going to get a frog."

Digby waited while ReeCee parked her broom in the broom rack. When she rejoined him, he put his hand on her shoulder. "Today just might . . . "

" . . . be that day," she finished. They bumped fists and then

shoved their way into the general crush of kids pushing through the school's huge, arched doors.

Digby turned left towards his homeroom, while ReeCee let the crowd drag her along to the stairs leading to the tower.

It really was a tower, as the school was actually in a castle; the only castle in Williwog Woods. Unlike Fairy Tale Land, most Williwog residents lived in split-level crypts, ranch-style caverns, or the usual old, creaky houses described in every story beginning *It was a dark and stormy night.*

According to her Aunt Giddee, the castle had been built way long ago by some moldy, totally dead ancestor of the Frank N. Stynee family.

The heavy wooden door to the classroom was standing open when ReeCee got to the landing.

There were two rows with five desks each just inside the door. Although, this term, there were only seven students in the class. Five, if you counted the Stycks triplets as one witch in three bodies.

ReeCee put the box with the dust bunnies on Oliver's desk before slipping into her own, the one farthest from their special ed teacher, Mrs. Murgatroyd.

The whole perimeter of the room was filled with bookcases and cupboards holding hundreds of dusty, cobweb-covered books dotted with dead bug bodies. There were also all kinds of strange looking containers, wands, bones, and amulets from earlier times.

On the first day of class, Mrs. Murgatroyd had strictly forbidden them from touching anything on the shelves. "This is some of the oldest magic in Willwog Woods. It has been in my charge for eons. The mere fact that you are even allowed to breathe the same air in this room is more than any of you deserve. And if you touch anything, I will instantly turn you into a super-sized stench turd. Got it?"

The kids knew Mrs. Murgatroyd would do exactly that. She had been teaching longer than any other teacher in the school. ReeCee didn't really know how long that was, but Mrs. Murgatroyd had taught ReeCee's father when he was a student.

When she and her parents had attended the open house at the beginning of the school year, Mrs. Murgatroyd had looked Mr. Toadmite over carefully before saying, "Well, Aconite, I've seen the commercials for your broom store. I must tell you that I am totally amazed that a worthless, scholastic slug who was totally deficient in magic managed to become productive in society." She was then silent for one long, icy moment. "I see that you married Malady Longrack."

Mrs. Murgatroyd reached out to pat ReeCee's mother's arm. "I'm sorry, dear, I was hoping you would do better. That does, however, explain your daughter."

On their way home, her mom explained that Mrs. Murgatroyd absolutely terrified ReeCee's dad when he was in school.

"She still does," he had muttered.

By the end of her first day in class, ReeCee understood why.

CHAPTER 3

ReeCee looked over to where the ghost of her latest failure still haunted the project table and sighed. It was the first spell of the year, a spell so simple that she should have mastered it in second grade.

Mrs. Murgatroyd had sprinkled dirt on the round project table. She then gave each of them a slip of paper with the words to the spell. All they had to do was focus their intent, read the words properly, and the little bits of dirt would turn into flies. They didn't even have to memorize it or anything.

Oliver Offal had been the first to try it. The few flies he was able to conjure weren't very good. Actually, they were pretty terrible. Some had oversized eyes while others had too many legs, and some were really fat with teeny tiny heads. They only lasted a few seconds before popping back into dirt. At least they were sorta flies though, and since Oliver's magic skills were limited because he was an ogre, Mrs. Murgatroyd gave him an A.

The Stycks sisters went next. Hortuna, Hulga, and Hogatha were triplet witches with a single magic divided among them. In order for them to cast, they all had to focus on the same thing at the same time. Unfortunately, focusing wasn't something they did very well so they often ended up with some strange results from their spells. Holding hands, they had managed one single fly that was about the size of a quagmire lizard. Actually, it looked like a quagmire lizard with wings, but it did fly.

Mrs. Murgatroyd let it fly around the table a couple of times before she pointed a finger and it turned back into dirt. The sisters were given a B because it had wings and flew, even if it wasn't exactly a fly.

That left three students. Marvin Griffin, Bobby Stynee, and ReeCee.

Magic didn't run in Marvin's family. Their special skill set revolved around invisibility. Each member of the Griffin family could simply vanish at will. Each member, that is, except Marvin. Marvin—or rather parts of Marvin—came and went, but never all at once or completely. It could get really bizarre in class on those days when the only thing that disappeared was his brain.

Bobby Stynee didn't really need to be in special ed. He was totally on top of his game in both monstering and junior high football. However, like all the Stynees, he had to plug into a charging station regularly, which meant there was this constant electrified field around him. While it was pretty useful for stuff like blitzing bugs, it also blitzed eyeFones and computers.

When one of his teachers had asked Bobby to deliver something to the principal's office in the other tower of the castle, he'd wiped out all the school servers. Since Mrs. Murgatroyd prohibited electronics of any kind in the special ed room, Bobby got stuck in it.

That had made it ReeCee's turn. She spent a moment focusing on her intent, then carefully read the words on the slip Mrs. Murgatroyd had given before pointing her finger.

Nothing happened.

After a few moments, Mrs. Murgatroyd sighed and told her to try it again.

Suddenly, the little bits of dirt began to hop up and down, swirling around and around. Finally, they had all exploded into what looked suspiciously like gumdrops. In a few minutes, there was a huge pile on the table as every bit of the dirt transformed.

What was not on the table was a single wing or fly leg. And the only thing with huge eyes was Mrs. Murgatroyd.

ReeCee froze, clutching her spell paper.

"Those are not flies, ReeCee," Mrs. Murgatroyd had said. "Would you like to tell me what they are?"

Oliver picked up one that had tumbled in his direction and popped it into his mouth (Note: ogres have a pretty cast-iron constitution when it comes to eating strange stuff.). "Chocolate gumdrops, Mrs. M.," he said, reaching for another.

"Don't touch them," she commanded.

Mrs. Murgatroyd leveled her finger at the pile and, muttering a spell under her breath, fired it.

Nothing happened.

She tried it again. Still nothing. She studied her finger for a moment and tried it for the third time. The gumdrops neither moved nor transformed back into dirt.

Mrs. Murgatroyd had then reached inside her robe and pulled out her wand.

Wands were something students weren't allowed to use. After a couple of close calls, a campaign had been mounted to keep wands out of the elementary and middle schools. Using the motto, *It's all fun and games until somebody's head gets blown off,* concerned parents

had persuaded the school board to prohibit the use of wands until children entered high school.

Mrs. Murgatroyd tapped the pile with her wand and a wave of light washed over the table. When it faded, the gumdrops remained.

While the class was staring at the stubborn pile, a strange grinding noise had begun. Looking around the room, the students finally realized it was coming from Mrs. Murgatroyd. Her jaws were moving back and forth, side to side.

Even though all that could be currently seen was his left hand and right eyeball, Marvin asked, "Ummm, can we get you something, Mrs. Murgatroyd?"

She answered by stumping to and opening the cupboard that stood between the two windows. She pulled out a gray bottle labeled "Slug Broth for Locked Jaws." She took a healthy swallow and sat down. "I had not had an attack of lockjaw in a hundred years," she said. "Now, I have lockjaw." She took another swig from the bottle.

With everyone watching their teacher, Oliver had quietly reached back to sneak a handful of the gumdrops. The movement triggered a feeding frenzy. The rest of the students started grabbing and stuffing them into their mouths, pockets, and school bags.

ReeCee had dropped a couple of handfuls into her witch bag to give to Digby later. Chocolate was Digby's favorite flavor of blood.

CHAPTER 4

Now, though, ReeCee wished she hadn't eaten her breakfast of bog-berry pancakes. Worry about messing up today's magic was chewing at her stomach like crypt beetles.

Oliver lumbered in and spotted the box on his desk. "Is that for me, ReeCee?" he asked.

She nodded. "More dust bunnies."

He grabbed the box and headed back to the door, "Gonna stash these so Mrs. M. doesn't think I've been touching stuff. Be right back."

"Hey, watch it!"

"Sorry, Marv, didn't see you."

"Really?" Marvin asked excitedly.

"Well, most of you."

ReeCee watched Marvin's left elbow, lower right leg, and both feet sit down at his desk. Maybe Marvin couldn't quite control his invisibility, but at least he didn't have to worry about screwing up magic spells.

While she was looking at Marvin, an unfamiliar voice spoke behind them, causing both kids to jump.

"Hullo, is this Mrs. Murgatroyd's classroom?"

"Yes, it is," Marvin answered as he and ReeCee turned toward the door.

A man dressed very much like a fairy tale prince hesitated in the doorway. He was peering carefully in the direction of Marvin's desk, trying to see who had answered him.

ReeCee looked at him curiously. It wasn't often a fairy tale denizen came over to the nightmare side of Williwog Woods.

A little geyser of glee rose in her. Edweena was going to be sooooo jealous if he really was a prince.

Edweena was totally addicted to fairy tale reality shows like *Poison Apple Green*, *Tress Tower*, and *The Real Dancing Princesses of Bling Hills*.

ReeCee never understood why watching a bunch of princes rescue someone silly from something sillier just so they could look heroic was such a big deal. Seriously, how does fighting off a green-gilled guppie even count as 'hero' work? Plus, every show always ended with the same totally drippysap happily-ever-after.

The man didn't actually look much like the princes on those shows, though he was dressed similarly. He was short and squat with bulgy eyes and a wide, almost lipless mouth. His nose was flattish while his blonde hair, hanging down from under his cap, was kinda weedy.

As she studied him, she was startled when she realized he was studying her right back. "Are you a fairy?" he asked.

ReeCee's cheeks burned hot. She hated it when someone pointed out her skin was rosy and pink instead of green.

"Nah," Marvin answered. "ReeCee's a witch."

"Are you sure? Her nose is rather pert for being a witch."

Marvin's left shoulder, which had just popped into view, shrugged. "Well, she's just kinda not good at it."

ReeCee huffed under her breath. Marvin had a lot of room to talk.

The man abruptly hopped to the right when the three Stycks sisters clattered through the door. They stopped and looked him over, tilting their heads in thought.

"Prince Charming," Hortuna said.

He shook his head. "No, that's my oldest brother."

"Prince Dashing?" Hulga asked.

He shook his head again. "That's my second brother."

"Then you must be Prince Gallant," Hogatha stated.

"That's my third brother."

Oliver, who returned to the room while the three sisters were guessing, spoke. "Come on. Everyone knows he's Prince Valiant."

The man sighed and, again, shook his head. "No, that's my mother's cousin twice removed on my grandfather's side. I am Prince Bufoo of Mishmush," he said with a deep bow.

Just then, one of the windows opened and Mrs. Murgatroyd swooped in.

The students hastily threw themselves into their desks and began pulling out notebooks and pencils, trying to look like they were ready and eager for the day.

Mrs. Murgatroyd set a shopping bag on her desk while her broom lofted itself to settle into its rack above the cupboard between the two windows.

Then she officially started the class by giving them her morning scary witch squint.

Her eyes unsquinted when she spotted Prince Bufoo standing at the back of the room. She gave him a smile that was almost as scary.

"Students, as you hopefully remember, we are going to be working on our 'prince–into-frog' spell this morning. Prince Bufoo of Mishmush has generously offered to be the prince."

The prince limply lifted a hand. "Actually, you are doing me a favor. I haven't had the best of luck getting a maid to agree to become the other half of my happily-ever-after." His voice trailed off glumly. "I thought I might have a bigger pool to choose from if I was a frog prince," he said, looking back at the kids.

Mrs. Murgatroyd cleared her throat. "Ummmm, yes, thank you, Prince Bufoo." She reached into the shopping bag and pulled out a box. Carrying it to one the project tables, she took the lid off, carefully tilting it until a frog hopped out.

"Now, this is what the prince should look like after you have cast your spell. Nice and green, with the proper number of legs, feet, and toes. I don't want scales, fangs, or claws, got it? Give me a dragon, and you're going to get a D to match. Give me a flame-throwing dragon, and it's an F. Okay, Prince Bufoo, if you would please just hop up on the other table."

"Now, before we begin, I want you to watch this excellent BooTube video that demonstrates exactly how to cast the perfect prince-to-frog spell." She snapped her fingers and a flat-screen crystal ball appeared. Another snap and the video began.

ReeCee paid close attention, trying to memorize the exact motions and words. She hoped that Mrs. Murgatroyd would call on her first, before she forgot what to do.

CHAPTER 5

Instead, Mrs. Murgatroyd pointed at the Stycks sisters. "Girls, you go first."

Although they inhabited three completely separate bodies, they sometimes tried to move as one. This always led to flailing arms, entangled feet, and the potential for bodily injury to others who happened to be in the vicinity. Consequently, their approach to the table was chaotic. They finished their journey with a small shoving match as each of them jockeyed to be the one closest to Prince Bufoo. They stopped when Mrs. Murgatroyd went back into her witch squint.

When everyone was finally standing still, Mrs. Murgatroyd pointed her finger, and a hologram appeared with the words to the spell. "Hold hands and read the spell. After you read the words, cast through the hologram. It is very, very important that you do this in unison, girls, so do focus."

Each of the girls began to mouth the words as they read them. Within the first two words they were each reading at a different pace.

Two of the girls were still mouthing the words when Hogatha pointed her finger and cast. Hortuna finished and cast a second later. Hulga continued reading.

Prince Bufoo jumped as the magic hit him. In an instant, he had two hind frog legs courtesy of Hogatha. Hortuna's spell turned him neon green. When Hulga finally finished and pointed her casting finger, an enormously long tongue popped out of the Prince's mouth.

"Mmmmph, mmphhhh, mmpppph." The Prince flapped his arms and tried to talk.

Mrs. Murgatroyd quickly reversed the fractured spell. The Prince drew in a couple of deep breaths before speaking. "I hate to sound critical or ungrateful, but I do think it would be better if I was all frog. I have no idea where I would locate a half-frog, half-princess to woo."

Oliver was frantically waving his arm in the air.

"Yes, Oliver," Mrs. Murgatroyd said. "Do you want to give it a try?"

"If I manage to turn him into a frog, can I eat him?"

"We do not eat guests, Oliver," she said sternly. "Now who's next? Marvin? No. Bobby? No. Oliver? Definitely not. So I guess it's ReeCee's turn." Mrs. Murgatroyd said reluctantly.

ReeCee looked at the frog, the prince, and then focused on the words once again floating in a hologram. She read them carefully and, raising her hand, she cast through the words as Mrs. Murgatroyd had instructed.

At that precise moment, Prince Bufoo raised his hand to swat a fly circling his head. ReeCee's spell struck the large ruby ring on the prince's finger and a cloud of pink-smelling smoke erupted, temporarily obscuring both the prince and the frog, who had been hungrily eyeing the fly.

Mrs. Murgatroyd quickly waved her hands, pushing the smoke away from the table.

ReeCee's heart sank when she realized the prince looked quite as he had when he arrived that morning. There wasn't any frog to be seen anywhere on him. At least the Stycks sisters had managed some frog parts.

Everyone was looking at the prince who was still a prince, when Oliver spoke. "Hey, Mrs. M., the frog isn't on the table any more. If I find it, can I have it for lunch?"

"Who's that under the table?" Bobby asked.

Mrs. Murgatroyd bent over to look under the table. Crouched on the floor, a young woman dressed in pale pink lace and ruffles was looking around in confusion. Straightening up, Mrs. Murgatroyd closed her eyes and began drawing in and blowing out deep breaths.

Leaning over the edge, the prince peeked under the table. He immediately leapt to the floor and, taking her hand, helped the girl out, where he stared at her for a very long moment. She, too, was short and squat with a wide, almost lipless mouth. There was the faintest cast of green to the curls cascading down her back.

You're . . . you're beautiful," the prince gasped as he looked into her bulging blue eyes.

She smiled at him and tried to speak. It came out a rather garbled croak. She coughed and tried again. "Sorry, I seem to have a little frog left in my throat."

"ReeCee, you turned my lunch into a princess," Oliver said accusingly.

The prince dropped to one knee and holding both her hands started to ask, "Will you do me the honor of becoming my—" He stopped suddenly and stood up.

"My dear Mrs. Murgatroyd, will she stay this way? The spell won't wear off, will it?" Prince Bufoo asked. "I mean, I don't want

to be in the middle of our wedding when, poof, she suddenly turns back to a frog."

"Somehow I suspect she will stay as she is, but I will run a spell check to be sure the magic won't unravel," Mrs. Murgatroyd said in a pinched voice.

She pulled her wand out and muttered a princess-into-frog chant. A puff of green popped in the air. When it disappeared, the girl still stood there.

"Splendid," the prince said as he again dropped to one knee and completed his proposal. The frog princess shyly nodded her acceptance.

The prince then turned to ReeCee who was trying very hard to make herself invisible. "Although your classmates insist that you are a witch, I must tell you that I will always think of you as the fairy who granted my dearest wish. I shall see you receive an invitation to the wedding. You will always be a welcome and honored guest in Mishmush, should ever you have reason to visit Fairy Tale Land."

Then, hand in hand, the prince and princess headed out the door to their happily-ever-after.

Mrs. Murgatroyd's witch squint was blacker than ever when she fixed it on ReeCee. "I have a headache. No student in the history of Williwog Woods Consolidated Public School has ever given me a headache. You, ReeCee, have given me a headache."

***

Digby was waiting for ReeCee at the bottom of the stairs when school let out.

"Well?" he asked as soon as she appeared.

"I turned a frog into a princess and gave Mrs. Murgatroyd a headache," she answered.

"So, I'm guessing today wasn't 'that day'?"

"Ya think?" ReeCee said as she retrieved her broom.

31

CHAPTER 6

Two brooms were parked by the open front door of ReeCee's house. A large brown spider was sitting on the handle of one, sunning himself in the afternoon warmth.

"Hi, Bosco," ReeCee said as she stopped to lightly stroke the back of her aunt's favorite spider. Lifting a leg in greeting, the spider hitched his abdomen to the left so ReeCee could tickle his favorite spot.

"Let me see if I can figure out who the other broom belongs to," Digby said.

Heart stickers with the name Beau glowing in each one covered the handle of the broom.

ReeCee groaned.

As ReeCee and Digby stepped into the house, several boxes were gliding down the stairs and into the living room. The kids dodged them and headed to the kitchen for their after school snacks.

Once ReeCee had a handful of weevil wafers and Digby the blood drops his mother had sent over, they wandered into the living room. Old decorations that had been used for promotions at her dad's store spilled out of boxes stacked around the floor.

Aunt Giddee and ReeCee's mother were sorting through the boxes and making piles of streamers, glittery balls, and other items.

"So what do you need?" ReeCee's mom asked.

Sitting on the couch checking messages on her eyeFone, Edweena shrugged petulantly, "I don't know. The whole stupid Dragon in the Dungeon thing is so lame anyway. I mean, why does there have to be some smelly old lizard running around a dance?"

"It's tradition," ReeCee's mom said. "There's been a Dragon in the Dungeon dance since before your mom and I were in school."

"The dragon blows the smoke that makes it all shadowy and mysterious," Aunt Giddee answered.

"That is just so last millennia, Mom. They have instant smoke now. You just open it up and poof . . . smoke. You can even get it in shimmer, glitter, crystalline, any color you want."

"Maybe, but then Elliot and Sparkle would be out of a job they very much need," ReeCee's mother said.

"Yeah, who names a dragon 'Sparkle' anyway? And why does a troll even have a dragon? I thought wizards were the only ones who could have dragons."

ReeCee's mother looked at her sister, "Hasn't Edweena heard the story about Elliott and Sparkle?"

"Oh really, Malady, that is such a sad story," Giddee said.

Edweena rolled her eyes and sighed heavily to emphasize her total lack of interest, but ReeCee and Digby eagerly responded. "We haven't heard the story either. Tell us!" and they quickly flopped on the floor.

Ignoring her sister, ReeCee's mother began. "Well, it actually started a very long time ago. Before your father, Giddee, or myself were born, when all dragons were under the control and protection of the Ancient Grand Wizard Anjar. It was his responsibility to ensure that every dragon hatched was strong, healthy, and suited to its purpose. As such, it was also part of his job to gather and destroy any eggs that were deformed or damaged in order to protect the dragon lines and their heritage."

"You mean he killed baby dragons?" Digby asked. "That's horrible!"

"Yes, it does sound horrible, but the eggs were actually destroyed before they became baby dragons. Remember, only the fiercest of dragons could survive. Even if Anjar had not destroyed the eggs, the smaller, weaker dragons would have been killed by their stronger siblings. It really was kinder to dispose of an egg before it became a baby dragon.

"Anyway, that particular season, the Wizard found an egg in one of the nests that, although perfectly formed, was much, much smaller than the rest. He removed it, placing it with others that would be taken to the place where they were ritually destroyed.

"What Anjar didn't realize, however, was that living in the area designated for egg destruction was a young troll who had run away from his family, taking only his clothes and an old cooking pot."

"Was it Elliott?" ReeCee asked.

Her mother nodded. "Yes, it was."

"Why did Elliott run away? Was his family mean to him?" Digby asked.

Again, ReeCee's mother nodded. "Yes, and not just his family. Pretty much all the trolls were mean to him. You see, as far as the trolls were concerned, Elliott was defective."

"Defective? What was wrong with him?" ReeCee asked.

35

"He had been born cute."

"Cute?" ReeCee and Digby said together.

"Yes. Cute. And since trolls pride themselves on being the ugliest residents in Williwog Woods, life was very hard for Elliott. When he didn't get uglier as he got older, he ran away. He wandered around until he found a snug little cave in the side of the Sogslog Mountains. And that is where Sparkle ended up in Elliott's pot of boiling soup."

A maniacal laugh erupted in the room. ReeCee's mom began to push aside the various piles of decorations. "Does anyone know where my phone is?" she asked.

CHAPTER 7

"This story is getting horribler," Digby said, looking at ReeCee. She nodded her head in agreement.

"That was your dad. He's waiting for a shipment and will be late coming home tonight. Now, where was I?"

"The baby dragon was being boiled in Elliott's soup," Digby said.

"Well, not really since Sparkle was still an egg. See, Ancient Anjar would carry the eggs to the very top of Sogslog at the beginning of winter. It is very cold up there. Dragon eggs need tremendous heat for the leathery shells to harden and baby dragons to hatch; they cannot survive when it's even a little cold, let alone very, very cold."

She paused as she pulled a silvery spider out of a box. It scuttled under the couch when she set it on the floor. "Remind me to gather it back up when we're done here."

"Hmmmm, 'very, very cold'—," ReeCee said.

"Yes, cold. So anyway, Anjar was climbing to the top of the mountain and somehow on the way, he dropped the little egg. It apparently rolled and bounced down the side of Sogslog until it landed in the pot of soup Elliott was cooking outside his cave. That boiling water acted just like a parent dragon's hot breath and, when Elliott fished the egg out, it was ready to hatch. The egg split apart, and a very small dragon emerged.

"Despite knowing it was against all the rules to keep the dragon, Elliott also knew that Sparkle would be destroyed because of her size. Besides, he was very lonely living by himself in that little cave, so he kept and raised her. Although he tried to stay hidden from the endless eyes of Williwog Woods, it was inevitable that one creature or another would see them and report back to others. Eventually, stories started going around about a troll who didn't look like a troll and lived with a small dragon.

"When word reached Anjar, he offered a very nice reward for whoever could prove the stories were true by finding them. Elliott must have heard about the reward because he and Sparkle disappeared for a very long time.

"Eventually, the time came when Anjar was called into the mists. Without a formal keeper, the dragons dispersed to other lands of myth and legend. Then one day, Elliott and Sparkle showed back up in Williwog Woods. It was evident that their time elsewhere hadn't been easy. And although this was their home, the trolls were no more welcoming to Elliott. Although no longer cute, he had not aged into ugliness.

"There were still many who remembered the dragons of old, so Elliott and Sparkle were able to make a living appearing at different events. That was when someone got the idea for the first Dragon in the Dungeon dance. I remember going with your father, ReeCee. It was so romantic dancing in Sparkle's smoky breath." Her mom's voice went soft with memory.

"But all things change, and the old memories faded. Elliott and Sparkle have ended up trying to eke out a living by burning trash piles, smoking out vermin, and making appearances at the odd event like the Dragon in the Dungeon dance.

"And that, Edweena, is why although there are other ways to create smoke nowadays, Elliott and Sparkle are still used at the dance."

"Well, it's still dumb," Edweena grumped. "If the school wasn't wasting money on that old dragon, then there would be money to buy some super-cool decorations instead of using leftovers from Uncle Aconite's store."

Now there was an edge to her Aunt Malady's's voice. "You know, Edweena, you can still go shopping, if that would make you feel better. If not, maybe you could tell your mom and me exactly what colors you want."

"How about these nice orange ones, darling," Giddee said holding up some streamers that shimmered like pale fire.

"Really, Mom? You want me to look like I'm part of the decorations.?"

Giddee looked at her daughter with a puzzled expression.

"Mom, my dress is orange, remember? And I don't even want to do the stupid decorations anyway. I just signed up because some lying skink told me Beau was on the committee."

ReeCee elbowed Digby, jerking her head in the direction of her bedroom.

"How can Edweena not care about the hard life that Elliott and Sparkle have lived," ReeCee said as she plopped down on the edge of her bed while Digby sprawled on the floor.

"I'm pretty sure she gives spiders the creeps," he said.

A series of squeaks came from above the window where Ree-Cee's little bat, Beatrice, was hanging.

"See, Beatrice said Edweena scares the hiss out of her, too," Digby said.

"I really wish I could see Sparkle and Elliott. I don't know why only seventh and eighth graders get to go to the dance. I just hope they are still doing the Dragon in the Dungeon dance when I get to be a seventh grader. Unless Mrs. Murgatroyd decides to turn me into a toadstool, gargoyle, or whatever."

Digby shook his head decisively. "You don't have to wait two more years. You can see them next Friday at a special reception they're holding at the school."

"What reception?"

"This year is the 50th anniversary of the Dragon in the Dungeon dance, so the school is going to do something special for Elliott and Sparkle. You can see them then!"

"How come you know about the reception and I don't?"

"Duh, Dalen and Derry." Digby reminded ReeCee about the Noktern twins who were in the eighth grade.

"Oh yeah, I kinda forget about your brother and sister since I hardly ever see them."

"Plus Mom and Dad are chaperoning, so I think my mom is gonna ask your mom if I can hang out here while everyone is at the dance."

"That would be cool. Maybe Mom will let us make some cara-mel-covered flies!"

Beatrice did a happy little swoop around the room. She loved caramel-covered flies

CHAPTER 8

Friday had felt forever away. ReeCee worried every second that she was going to do something stupid and not be allowed to attend the event for Elliott and Sparkle. When Friday arrived, she practically held her breath all day. Finally though, Principal Haydeez's voice came over the intercauldron requesting that all students assemble in the central hall to welcome Elliott and Sparkle.

Mrs. Murgatroyd ordered the students to clean up their desks and then line up single file. Slipping her witch bag over her shoulder, ReeCee took her place at the very end of the line. She was so excited it was hard to stand still, but Mrs. Murgatroyd would keep them there all night if anyone so much as twitched.

Finally, Mrs. Murgatroyd opened the classroom door and led them down the twisting stairs from the tower to the main floor where Principal Haydeez was endeavoring to impose some order on the mass of milling students.

Magically, though, everyone fell into place when the great door opened revealing the outline of a man and a dragon's humpback backlit by the fall sun.

Principal Haydeez hurried toward the pair in welcome.

Although he didn't look like a troll, Elliott was dressed as one. The thick walking stick he carried banged in time to his steps. He frowned and glared at the kids as he stumped along behind the principal. Sparkle was truly a very small dragon. She was barely taller than Elliott. She walked slowly as if she was very tired.

Just looking at the two, ReeCee understood what her mother had meant about time not being kind to them. Between his raggedy clothes and faded gray eyes, there was definitely a worn look to Elliott. Time had also muted Sparkle's rosy coloring. Her eyes held a patient sadness as she followed the troll. It pinched ReeCee's heart.

They were passing her class when Sparkle nudged Elliott out of the way, stopping right in front of ReeCee. The dragon's breath was tremendously warm as it washed over her. Sparkle didn't seem so small now as she towered over the girl while sniffing her.

"Whatcha got in there, girl," Elliott asked as he gestured toward her bag with his stick.

"Carrionberry muffins," ReeCee stammered. "Two them. Would you like them?" she asked.

"Not me," Elliott said, "but Sparkle here has a real taste for carrionberries." He gently stroked the dragon's neck. "She doesn't get them as often as she deserves."

ReeCee lifted her bag over her head and, setting it on the floor, she fished out the muffins.

"Uh, Mr. Elliott, sir, you might not wanna to do that," Marvin said.

"Who said that?" Elliott said as he looked up and down the line of students. "Show yourself."

Marvin stepped out of line. "I mean, ReeCee's my friend and all, but things get real weird when she is involved."

"I'm talking to a left elbow and right shin and you're telling me she's weird?"

Sparkle's breath began to get even warmer as she sniffed the muffins ReeCee held in each hand.

"Go ahead, girl, give 'em to her, but be careful. Like all dragons, she can snap when excited."

Sparkle, however, was a perfect lady as she carefully took the muffins from ReeCee and happily swallowed them.

Elliott turned to continue down the hall. Sparkle blew out one more warm breath before following him.

ReeCee's heart felt better.

CHAPTER 9

It was quiet in the Toadmite house. ReeCee and Digby were propped up on either end of the sofa. Digby was concentrating on drawing another panel for his comic book while ReeCee was slowly leafing through her mother's newest *Bone Appetite* magazine. Beatrice was hanging upside down from a figurine on the coffee table, happily licking up the remains of the caramel-covered flies the kids had made earlier.

The quiet shattered when a piercing wail was suddenly heard coming from outside the house.

"What is that banshee shrilling about now?" Giddee asked.

"I'm not sure that's the banshee," ReeCee's mom said, cocking her head toward the door as she listened.

ReeCee and Digby looked at each other and rolled their eyes. "Edweena."

Giddee jumped up and hurried to the door. Before she reached it, it flew open and a howling Edweena flung herself into the entry hall.

49

She was covered in what looked like cobwebs.

"Good graves, Edweena, what is that," her mother asked as she touched the material.

"It's from that stupid dragon. Instead of smoke, he was blowing snot everywhere . . . on the food, the decorations, people!"

"She," ReeCee said. "Sparkle is a girl."

Lou and Crezia Noktern fluttered for a moment in the doorway before transforming. "Isn't that amazing," Lou said as he plucked a piece of the web-like material from Edweena's dress.

This elicited another wail from Edweena, who hurled herself into the living room and onto the sofa with all the drama of a dying ghoul.

ReeCee's mom took the fluttering bit from Lou. She ran it through her fingers, gently tugging and stretching it. She then lightly pulled it across the back of her hand.

"I haven't seen or felt anything like this since the eider spiders crawled off to Fairy Tale Land," she said.

He nodded. "Exactly. If I hadn't seen this come from the dragon, I would have bet my last pint of blood that it was from the spiders."

ReeCee and Digby looked at each other. They had no idea what their parents were talking about.

With no one rushing to comfort her, Edweena ratcheted up the volume on her sobs.

ReeCee and Digby edged farther from Edweena and closer to the adults.

"What are eider spiders?" Digby asked.

"A very long time ago, when all of us were little," Digby's dad motioned to all the adults, "the forest was filled with these big spiders." He held his hands out to indicate a size about that of an ogre's head. "The spiders spun webs out of some of the silkiest, shimmeriest, softest strands that ever were."

"They were definitely the web masters," Aunt Giddee said nodding.

"The odd thing about the spiders was that they spent all night hard at work weaving these very elaborate webs and at the first light of dawn, they gathered them up, pitching them to the forest floor before going to bed," ReeCee's mom said.

"My dad, Digby's grandpa, would collect the webs. He thought they were too amazing to just pile up around the trees. After a lot of experimentation, he figured out how to untangle the webs and reweave the strands into cloth. He then used the material he wove to make the capes, shawls, and cloaks he sold. That was the main reason that Noktern's Natty Night and Day Wear became the go-to place for all your outerwear needs."

"Did something happen to the spiders?" ReeCee asked.

"Well, before there were eyeFones, eekmail, websights, and all that other technology, people used to travel back and forth from Williwog Woods and Fairy Tale Land to conduct business and make trades. You know, buy and sell stuff," Giddee explained.

"One evening when a tradesman from Fairy Tale Land was coming to do business, he was making his way through the forest just at dusk. This was exactly the time of day that the eider spiders came out and started their nightly web-weaving," Digby's mom said.

"They scared the pea-wadding out of him because of their size, so he started throwing some of the food he had brought with him, hoping that would keep them from eating him."

"They ate people?" Digby asked.

"Actually, no. They preferred very sweet things, like flowers, tree sap, and fruit flies."

Giddee added in. "The snacks the tradesman tossed at them were made from a plant that only grows in Mallow Marsh over in Fairy Tale Land. It's some kind of white, gooey, floofy stuff. Don't care for it myself."

"Me neither. There's just no bite to it," Digby's dad said. "However, the spiders did like it. Liked it so much that when the tradesman came back through, they followed him over the border. And, once all those princesses in Fairy Tale Land discovered just how beautiful the material was when the webs were untangled and woven, there has never been any question of finding a way to lure the eider spiders back to Williwog Woods."

"Do you think these smoke webs from Sparkle might work the same way?" ReeCee's mom asked.

"I sure am hoping they will."

"I wonder why Sparkle started blowing this out instead of smoke," Giddee asked thoughtfully.

"I don't really know," Digby's dad answered. "Maybe it's something that dragons do when they start getting old. Regardless, I just hope she keeps it up. Because if this stuff works out like I think it might, I intend to buy every bit of what Sparkle produces and that will mean Elliott and Sparkle will be able to live comfortably the rest of their days."

"And Sparkle can have all the carrionberries she wants," ReeCee told Digby.

A high-pitched sobbing shriek came from the couch. "Doesn't anybody here care at all that Beau didn't even ask me to dance once?"

Looking toward the front room, ReeCee and Digby yelled. "Nope."

***

The next day, ReeCee and Digby were sitting in ReeCee's backyard. She was gently tipping dust bunnies from her bedroom out of a box. The wind scuttled them into hiding among the leaves collecting under the trees.

"So Oliver doesn't want any more of them?" Digby asked from the shelter of his enormous umbrella. Although Digby tolerated the sun much better than most vampires, he still had to be careful how long he was in it. Too much time and he would fry. Literally.

"He said he has all he needs for his project."

She sat for a long time staring at the leaves where they could hear the dust bunnies rustling around. Finally, she asked, "Do you think I did something that changed Sparkle's smoke to that stuff your dad showed us last night?"

"How could you have? You had never even seen Sparkle until they came to the school yesterday."

"Well, I did give her the carrionberry muffins."

Digby shrugged "So? Elliott said you could."

"I helped Mom make those muffins."

"What do you mean you helped make those muffins?" Digby asked cautiously.

"Well, I stirred them . . . "

"Stirring can't hurt anything."

"With my magic," ReeCee finished.

Digby stared at her. "Let's not tell Dad about this," he said finally.

CHAPTER 10

ReeCee was feeling apprehensive as she climbed to the classroom. Tomorrow was Halloween; the biggest day of the year in Williwog Woods. The day the whole town prepared for all year.

As always, her dad had decorated the store from top to bottom in preparation for his annual "Knock You Alive Super Sale!" Across the street from the Toadmite Broom Store, Digby's dad would unveil his new fashion line at a special midnight showing.

Tomorrow was also an official school holiday. Instead of classes, students would help decorate and set up the gym and cafeteria for the annual Halloween Carnival in the evening.

Since a lot of parents from Williwog Woods were scheduled to put in appearances at locations in the human world, the school always staged a big event to keep the kids busy and safe until their parents returned.

Long-standing tradition required each class to create and provide part of the night's spooky atmosphere. ReeCee knew that

Digby's class was making replicas of some of the oldest tombstones in Williwog Woods, complete with mold, slime, and eyeballs, and Edweena had been totally excited that her class had raised enough money with their used body part sale to hire a troop of skeletons to scare up some fun.

But so far there had been no indication what the special ed class might be contributing. A bright, little thought popped to the forefront of her brain. Maybe, because they were special ed, they weren't going to be required to contribute to the event. That thought cheered her for the brief time it took her to reach the door.

As soon as she entered the classroom, ReeCee's stomach knotted.

The project table was set up with five cauldrons. Little trays with different colored goop sat in front of each one.

She hadn't realized that she actually stopped dead still until Oliver said, "Move it, Toadmite," and gave her a shove. Crossing to her desk, she slid in and slumped down. Yay . . . another chance to screw things up.

When everyone was finally seated, Mrs. Murgatroyd rapped on the skull on her desk for their attention while the lizard that lived in it hissed, "Husssssh." Rumor had it that the skull had belonged to a student who had pushed Mrs. Murgatroyd's buttons once too often.

"As you know, tomorrow is Halloween. This was once the most sacred of holidays in Williwog Woods. It was the night the most potent potions were brewed, the longest lasting hexes were inflicted, and the most powerful of spells were cast." She stared for a moment into that past while the kids just stared blankly at her.

"But, of course, it's all commercial now. Microwave-a-wand potions, just-add-hate hexes, and 'there's a-zapp-for-that' spells. The magic being cast today is completely pathetic; a ghost of what it once was. Everyone has become so dependent on their electronic devices that if there is ever a Wood-wide blackout, you all will be doomed, and not just to boredom." Sighing, she shook her head and then fixed a harsh squint on the class.

"It appears that my request to not have my students participate in the silly party magic that is taking place all over this school has been most firmly denied." She hitched a shoulder in irritation. "So students, today we have been tasked with making some enchanted balloons for tomorrow night."

She walked over to the table. "Since I will not waste my time teaching such idiotic skills, I have arranged everything so all you have to do is pour the ingredients on the trays into the cauldrons and stir them seven times. Not any more or any less. When you have completed that task, please step back. Precisely one minute after you have finished, a balloon will grow out of your cauldron. We will then tie them to the strings on the other table. I will enchant them myself."

Marvin was frantically waving the only part of himself that was visible in the air. Fortunately, it was his hand. "But, Mrs. Murgatroyd, I don't do magic."

"From what I have observed so far this school year, none of you 'do' magic," Mrs. Murgatroyd replied as she fixed a squint on Ree-Cee. "However, this particular project does not require any magic. You simply have to be able to pour in the ingredients and stir seven times. I do believe even Oliver can actually count to seven."

ReeCee let her breath out. At last, a project that she couldn't mess up. She absolutely could pour the goop into the cauldron and stir seven times. Her heart did a happy skip. Today might actually be "that day" Digby was always telling her was going to happen.

They were all called to the table at the same time. Mrs. Murgatroyd arranged the students in front of the cauldron she had designated for them. The Stycks sisters had one side of the table for themselves.

"Hortuna, Hulga, and Hogatha, please pay attention. You are to proceed exactly as I instruct. Hulga, you are to pour the material into the cauldron. Hogatha, you are to stir the mixture four times, then you are to let Hortuna take the spoon and proceed to stir the mixture three times only. Do not remove the spoon from the cauldron when you pass it, just let your sister take the handle.

It went pretty well even though Hogatha stirred only three times and Hortuna had to be reminded to give one more stir to meet the seven stirs requirement.

They stepped back when Mrs. Murgatroyd motioned, and, sure enough, at the end of one minute, a balloon shaped like a bat rose out of their cauldron.

"Me next, me next," Oliver begged, but Mrs. Murgatroyd shook her head. "We will go around the table in the order that I assigned you. That means that Marvin is next."

Since the only part of Marvin that could be seen now were his legs, the tray looked like it was rising mystically from the table. Once all the goop was tipped in, the spoon floated up and started to stir. Marvin very carefully counted as he completed each full stir of the cauldron. When he reached seven, the spoon rose out of the pot and settled on the table. At the sixty second mark, a spider balloon bobbed out.

In turn, Oliver stirred up a slimy toadstool, and Bobby got a very satisfactory black cat. Only one cauldron remained to bring forth its creation.

It was the very first time since the third grade that she felt pretty confident. If the Stycks sisters could do it, then it should be a piece of cake for her.

She carefully tilted the ingredients into the cauldron and stirred precisely seven stirs before removing the spoon.

Her sixty seconds felt a lot longer than everyone else's, but finally a round edge appeared. In a moment, her balloon was hovering in the air.

"Hey," Oliver said, "that's pretty cool."

"What is that?" Mrs. Murgatroyd sounded like she was being strangled.

CHAPTER 11

"It's a smiley face, Mrs. M. I have one at home that I use all the time to scare my little sister," Oliver answered.

"It is not supposed to be a 'smiley face'. It is supposed to be a jack-o'-lantern. How did you manage to turn the ingredients for a jack-o'-lantern into that?"

Not only was the balloon not a jack-o'-lantern, it seemed to be growing bigger than the other balloons. A lot bigger.

Marvin noticed. "Uh, is it supposed to be getting that big?"

Stunned by the balloon which had come out of the pot, their teacher had failed to notice that, indeed, the balloon was continuing to expand, and was now approaching the size of a dragon egg.

Mrs. Murgatroyd raised her hand and snapped her finger forward, firing off a deflation spell.

The balloon spun around as the blast of magic hit it. When it turned back to the classroom, its black line of a smile had circled around to frame an opening out of which air began to pour. As the air gushed out, the balloon began to spin. Faster and faster it went, creating a vortex.

The kids screamed and dove under the project tables. The balloon spun itself to the outside edge of the whirling air and began to sweep around the room, sucking up the huge accumulation of dust, cobwebs, and dead vermin that lay thickly over the ancient books and relics. When it had circled the entire room, it abruptly stopped. The air was instantly still and silent.

The kids peeked out from under the tables. The balloon was drifting slowly back and forth in front of Mrs. Murgatroyd's face, who still had her finger aimed in its direction. Then it bobbed backwards to the window, which was slowly opening behind it.

The balloon whipped around and spewed its contents out through the window. A huge cloud of dust shot into the clear air before quickly dissipating. It turned back, pursed its smiley black line and blew an enormous raspberry in the direction of Mrs. Murgatroyd before collapsing into a puddle of yellow on the window sill.

Mrs. Murgatroyd stared at it before glancing at the bookcase on her left. Her arm dropped as she turned in a very slow circle, staring at the bookcases. There was not a speck of dust; not a single dead bug body; not a cobweb to be seen. The shelves and their contents were ordered and immaculate.

Her own mouth shaped into an O that grew larger and larger. When she had turned all 360 degrees, she flung her arms out and her head back, letting loose a shriek that was, no doubt, frightening innocents in the far corners of Fairy Tale Land.

The kids dove for cover again, pressing their hands to their ears in an effort to shut out the dreadful cry.

It stopped as abruptly as the howling air had stopped.

Slowly, the kids unwrapped their arms from around their heads and peeked out from under the tables. Mrs. Murgatroyd was standing frozen, arms outstretched and head flung back, with her mouth still circled around a now silent scream.

Bobby crawled out from under the table first, followed by Oliver, and either Marvin or the Stycks sisters. No one was sure because, for the first time in his life, Marvin had completely disappeared. ReeCee got up on her hands and knees, but didn't leave the shelter of the table.

"Mrs. Murgatroyd, are you alright?" Bobby asked. He waved his hand in front of her eyes which were squinched shut.

Getting no response, he carefully held up a finger a few inches from the hooked end of Mrs. Murgatroyd's nose. *Bzzzt.* Electricity jumped between his finger and the teacher's nose with an audible snap. There was no reaction.

"Is she dead or something?" Marvin asked.

"Well, she is awfully old." Hortuna said while Hogotha and Hulga echoed, "old . . . old."

"You know, there's lots of different dead in Williwog. So I guess the question is she really, totally ding dong dead, or just kinda, sorta, maybe dead? And are we all gonna be turned into super stench turds when she undeads?" Oliver wondered.

ReeCee flopped over on her back. Unbelievably, she had not only managed to mess up a "no magic" project, but she might have killed their teacher.

"I think we better call the office and have them send over Mrs. Castorbeen," Marvin said.

"Yeah," Bobby nodded. "I don't know how long it takes for really dead witches to start stinking."

Oliver poked Mrs. Murgatroyd. "She's still soft. No rigor mortis yet."

Marvin went to the intercauldron that sat on a shelf in Mrs. Murgatroyd's cupboard. Picking up the small wand lying next to it, he struck the triangle etched on the front.

A stream of mist rose, and the school's secretary Mrs. Snaglkrum's face floated on its surface. "Yes, Mrs. Murgatroyd?"

"Uhhhh, this is Marvin Griffin up here in the Room of Doom, er, I mean the special education room. I think we need Mrs. Castorbeen or somebody. We're not sure, but Mrs. Murgatroyd maybe just died."

The secretary, who was always frightfully efficient, nodded, unperturbed by Marvin's statement. "Yes. I will send someone immediately. As you know, killing teachers is absolutely prohibited under the Williwog Woods Public School Rules of Conduct." The mist vanished.

It was only a matter of moments before Mrs. Castorbeen swooped into the room on her broom. She had just stepped off when Principal Haydeez materialized out of a puff of smoke.

"Okay, students, will everyone just step over here with me so Mrs. Castorbeen can work?" He moved to stand in front of the table ReeCee was lying under.

Mrs. Castorbeen did a quick check of Mrs. Murgatroyd. "I've seen worse," she said as she opened the small emergency bag on the back of her broom.

Principal Haydeez turned his attention to the children. "Can someone please tell me what was going on just prior to Mrs. Murgatroyd's sad demise?"

As the oldest in the room, Bobby started. "Well, we were making balloons for tomorrow's party. Everybody's balloon came out fine except ReeCee's. Instead of the jack-o'-lantern Mrs. Murgatroyd said it was supposed to be, it popped out of the cauldron a smiley face. Anyway, that made Mrs. Murgatroyd mad, so she zapped it."

"And then the balloon got mad." Oliver took over the story, "and it sucked up all the dust, cobwebs, bugs and other stuff that was on the shelves and spit it all out the window."

"It was at that point that Mrs. Murgatroyd had some kind

of attack. First, she screeched really, really long and loud. Then everything stopped, and she was just like you see her now," Marvin finished.

Principal Haydeez turned around and studied the room. "Oh, it has been cleaned, hasn't it?"

There was a collective intake of breath among the students. ReeCee closed her eyes. This was it. She was so going to be gargoyled.

"It looks splendid," he said, clapping his hands. "I have been trying to get Mrs. Murgatroyd to let us clean this room for centuries, but she was completely convinced that the dust and dead bugs were part of some ancient legacy. She even threatened to turn anyone, including me, into a . . . "

Mrs. Castorbeen had finished her poking and prodding. "Well, the good news is she isn't dead but rather torpored. A few weeks of rest and relaxation and she should be as right as rain."

"Torpored?" The kids looked at each other. Even ReeCee got back on her hands and knees to peer out at Mrs. Castorbeen.

"Yes, dears. Torpored. It's like a built-in kill switch. It happens if a witch's emotional state has reached the point where they are capable of doing real harm . . . such as blowing the school and everyone in it to smithereens. It puts them into a kind of involuntary hibernation and hopefully, when they untorpor, they have reconsidered their actions and decide not proceed."

"If you could lend a helping finger, Principal, I will just take her home and get her settled."

Principal Haydeez and Mrs. Castorbeen leveled their fingers at Mrs. Murgatroyd. In a moment, she was floating on her back in the air. Mrs. Castorbeen hopped on her broom and then, grabbing the back of Mrs. Murgatroyd's collar, she whisked them both out the window.

Their leaving caused the yellow balloon to slip off the ledge to the floor. Principal Haydeez went to pick it up.

"Was this the very bad little balloon that caused all the trouble?"

The kids looked at each other before nodding.

"Well, let's see if we can get it repaired. It has a party to go to! This smiley face just might be the scariest thing this school has seen in a long time."

CHAPTER 12

The rising harvest moon was very full as it began to peek over the battlements of the school.

"So, what do you want to do first?" Digby asked as he and ReeCee made their way toward the night's festivities.

"Eat! Mom and Dad were so busy at the store they didn't make it home for dinner, and I'm starving."

"Yeah. Dalen and Derry sucked up all the snacks Mom left and didn't leave me any. I told them it was gonna be their fault if I starved to death and Dalen just told me they weren't that lucky."

They got in line with the other students waiting to pass through the main door. Mrs.Snaglkrum was standing guard with her clipboard, checking off names before letting anyone in. The school was very careful about who passed through the doors, which were sealed with a special magic for this one night. Once someone entered, there was no leaving until dawn's first light or they were signed out by a parent or guardian.

Noise was already echoing through the castle when ReeCee and Digby were allowed in. They immediately headed to the cafeteria. Luckily, the line for food wasn't very long yet.

"Gosh, I hope they have blood pudding again this year." Digby said, licking his lips.

"I want a frankenfurter with pickled pigweed relish on it!"

After loading their food on trays, they were heading to a table when loud cackling erupted on one side of the room. It sounded eerily familiar.

Both kids glanced over as they put their trays on the table and swung their legs over the attached bench. Yup. Edweena, Zink, and Pym were standing together, witch giggling with their hands over their mouths, and working very hard to make sure they were noticed by another trio lounging on the other side of the room.

Looking where the girls were, the kids saw Beau Chomp, Larry Luppo and Digby's brother, Dalen, leaning against the opposite wall, being junior high cool.

ReeCee saw light glinting off of Dalen's mouth when he smiled.

"When did your brother get braces?" she asked.

"Last week. The orthodontist says he has a really bad cross-bite."

Then, ignoring both sides of the room, they focused on filling their very hungry stomachs.

Eventually, the three guys left, the three girls scrambling after them.

ReeCee shook her head as she popped the last bite of her frankenfurter into her mouth. "If I start acting that stupid when I'm twelve, bite me."

Digby had just leaned back and was happily patting his stomach when a fourth grader ran in and tagged another student.

"Hey, come on. Principal Haydeez just announced there's gonna be some kind of big surprise happening in the gym."

ReeCee and Digby looked at each other puzzled. Then ReeCee's eyes widened. "Maybe it's my balloon!"

They scrambled off the bench, pitching their garbage at the can as they raced out.

The gym was already filled almost to capacity with more students shoving their way in. Digby and ReeCee tried to maneuver their way through the taller students to a place where they could see.

Digby leaned over and yelled in her ear. "I think if we can get to the other side where the tombstones are, maybe you can climb up so you can see. Better grab my hand and hold on."

Gripping Digby's ice cold hand, ReeCee let herself be pulled through the warren of students.

A corner of the gym had been transformed into a temporary graveyard complete with tombstones.

"Oh, this IS cool," she said when Digby halted in front it.

"I think you can see if you stand on Marwick Ghoulish's stone."

"Who was he?"

"I don't know. Somebody dead dead."

"Where are you going to stand?"

"I'm not," Digby said, transforming into his bat form. He waved a wing at her before fluttering upward to hover above the crowd.

ReeCee climbed up on the tombstone and stood on tippy-toe to peer over the shoulders of the students milling in front of her. Suddenly, she could see what she guessed was the balloon hidden under a cover of black material floating above the crush of bodies. There was a distinct parting and reemerging of the crowd as someone pulled the balloon toward the center of the gym. She guessed it was Principal Haydeez, although she couldn't actually see him.

The balloon and Principal Haydeez stopped in the center of the room. She watched his hand reaching toward a corner of the cover over the balloon when suddenly all she could see were finger bones. One of the skeletons was messing with her.

She shoved the hands away. "Stop that! I'm trying to see!"

There was a soft clatter as the skeleton stepped away. ReeCee turned back as the cloth was being pulled ever so slowly from the balloon. The suspense growing in the room was palpable.

Just as the cloth began to slide off, bony fingers again covered her eyes. This time she angrily pushed the hands away, but it was too late. The shrieking and running feet let her know the moment was over. Yes, she could see her balloon smiling at everyone from the middle of the gym, but the stupid skeletons had ruined the actual unveiling.

She whirled around and pointed a finger at them. "Skeletons, be quick and shoo. Quit bugging me with your stupid games of boo. Get busy and do something useful for an hour or two."

The six skeletons looked at each other and then shrugged their white scapulae and wandered out of the graveyard.

Jumping down, ReeCee stepped out of the graveyard to wait for Digby. She was nearly trampled when Bobby and Oliver ran into her while bulling through the crowd, their heads together. They looked up, startled.

"Oh, hi, ReeCee. Good job on the balloon. Bobby and me, we got something to do. See ya," Oliver said.

Then with an evil snigger, he and Bobby shoved onward.

CHAPTER 13

"Hey, guys, come and see the cool skeletons we got." The voice behind ReeCee sent a shiver up her spine.

She did not want to have anything to do with her cousin, but she was also afraid if she left the graveyard, she and Digby wouldn't be able to find each other.

When Edweena, Zink, and Pym came into view, ReeCee was tickled to see that Zink's and Pym's noses had a more pronounced hook than Edweena's.

"And the skeletons are where?" Pym asked. "Because they aren't here."

"Who cares," Zink said. "Skeletons are so last Halloween. Besides, nothing could be scarier tonight than that yellow smiling balloon. I thought I was going to wet my pants when Principal Haydeez pulled the cover off."

Edweena nodded. "Yeah. I thought I was going to faint right into Beau's arms."

"That would have been a nice trick. He was on the other side of the room." Pym said cattily.

"Who brought the balloon, anyway?" Zink asked.

"We made it in Mrs. Murgatroyd's class," ReeCee piped up.

Edweena made a face at her. "You did not. Everyone knows that specks are too stupid to do magic. That's why they lock you up in the tower."

ReeCee made a face back at Edweena.

"I can make it freeze that way, and there won't be a thing you can do about it, speck." Edweena started to raise her hand.

Zink and Pym grabbed Edweena. "Come on, you're gonna get us sent to the detention room for the rest of the party if you cast without permission," they said, dragging her away.

ReeCee stuck her tongue out at Edweena's retreating back.

"Wow, I just saw the strangest thing!" Digby said as he walked up behind ReeCee.

"Jeeker kreakers, Digby, don't sneak up like that! You probably took a century off my life."

"Whatever. Anyway, it was kinda hot up there when I was watching the balloon, so I decided to go get a drink in the cafeteria. Guess who served me my blood orangeade?"

ReeCee shrugged. "I don't know."

"One of the skeletons that is supposed to be hanging out here in the graveyard. And not only that, but when I was coming back to the gym to find you, there was another one with a wastepaper basket picking up the stuff off the floor in the hall. Mrs. Snaglkrum was trying to get them back to the graveyard, but they just kept shaking their skulls while pointing to the clock. She thinks somebody was casting, which is like totally against the Carnival rules."

ReeCee buried her face in her hands.

"What?" Looking at ReeCee, Digby's eyes narrowed. "Did you do magic?"

"They kept putting their hands over my eyes when I was trying watch my balloon. I kinda lost my temper. Do you think Mrs. Snaglkrum can tell who cast?"

"Well, they're always saying that everybody's magic has its own special signature."

"I'm dead meat . . . again."

Just then, a little ogre girl walked up to the two older kids.

"Hi," she said. "My friends were wondering why you're that color," she pointed to ReeCee's face, "and not that color." The little girl pointed to a couple of other witch students standing on the edge of the graveyard. "Is it magic?"

"Aaarghhh!"

ReeCee ran from the gym. She raced through the area of the school designated for the Carnival, into the dark hall at the main entrance of the school, and up the steps leading to the second floor. At the top, she dove into the shadow created by a huge stone newel post.

She pulled her knees up tight to her chest and wrapped her arms around her legs. Roiling anger poured through her.

She hated skeletons; hated Mrs. Murgatroyd; hated Edweena; hated everything and everyone that kept reminding her she was too different and too stupid to be a real witch.

She was done, done, done with it all. She would stay here until the school doors opened. And she was never coming back to school again . . . ever. In fact, she was never going to see or talk to anyone else again. Maybe not even Digby. Hot tears welled up out of her very hurt heart.

In time, she was cried out and just sat with her forehead resting on her knees. The moon was slowly shifting through the sky and, when it emerged from behind the racing clouds, its light began to nibble away the edge of the dark space she huddled in. Sounds from the gym barely penetrated the musty air.

Suddenly ReeCee heard screaming . . . lots of screaming. She lifted her head for a moment. It must be time for the goodie drop, when the teacher witches opened a magic web in the gym so candy and other small hidden treats inside poured down. There was always lots of pushing and shoving as kids tried to grab the most.

ReeCee had learned a trick in the second grade when one of the bigger kids knocked her over. She just sat on the floor and grabbed things that came flying by as the kids kicked them around while running and chasing after everything. She had ended up with a nice, full bag and hadn't had to move at all.

She cocked her head and listened. The screaming was going on a lot longer than she remembered from previous years. Usually, once the candy fell, it was just yelling as the kids chased around.

Then she heard Digby whispering.

"ReeCee . . . ReeCee, are you in here?" The quiver in his voice let her know just how scared he was looking for her in the dark.

When she popped her head around the corner of the post, she could see Digby very slowing climbing the steps. "I'm here," she said.

Digby jumped about a foot at the sound of her voice and transformed. His wings were beating so fast she could feel the breeze they created on her face.

"Digby, quit being such a scaredy bat," she said. "You climb these stairs every day."

Digby transformed back into himself. "ReeCee, something terrible is happening! I think you are the only one who might know how to fix it."

ReeCee pulled back into the shadows. "Right," she said bitterly. "Find a real witch."

"Look, there is a twelve foot tall dust bunny rolling around in the gymnasium. It just ate Mrs. Snaglkrum!"

"It's not my problem. Besides, the teacher witches will zap it out of existence."

"They've been trying. It's not working. You're the only one that knows about these things."

"Yeah, and what makes you think I know something they don't?"

"You know how to clean," he said.

CHAPTER 14

"Yippee. I know how to clean. That isn't magic."

Digby put his face so close to hers their noses nearly touched. He spoke slowly, emphasizing each word. "It's. A. Dust. Bunny."

They stared at each other as comprehension came into ReeCee's blue eyes. "Do you really think I can?" she whispered.

"Today might be that day."

As they scrambled to their feet, they heard the sound of someone running in their direction. Beau Chomp was racing down the hall like Edweena was after him. He skidded to a stop at the foot of the stairs and looked around. He swung around to the window just as a cloud passed from in front of the full moon.

He clutched his hair with both hands and, arching back, began to howl.

"Terrific," Digby said. "Beau's gonna go all fur and fangs and take on the dust bunny."

But as the kids watched, something weird happened. Instead of bursting out of his clothes in a werewolf fury, Beau began to shrink until he vanished under the collapsing sweater and jeans.

ReeCee and Digby looked at each other in confusion. They slowly came down the stairs and squatted down on either side of the pile. There was movement in the clothes. In a moment, a werepuppy's head popped out. It opened its mouth in a fierce puppy-sized growl, revealing a rather unimpressive set of fangs.

Digby looked at ReeCee. "This is Edweena's hero?"

Suddenly, they heard the sound of lots of feet running in their direction. "Quick, Digby, take Beau and hide him upstairs."

Digby looked up the stairs. "It's dark up there," he said uncertainly.

"Don't worry, you have Beau to protect you."

"Riiight," Digby said as he gathered up the clothes-wearing werepuppy and headed reluctantly up the stairs.

ReeCee moved to stand in the middle of the hall. The flood of kids coming at her separated into channels as they raced around her. Behind them something huge was growling and roaring.

Digby was right. It was a dust bunny . . . a very, very, very large dust bunny. And it was getting closer.

ReeCee's heart began to pound. She couldn't do this. Today wasn't that day. She wanted to turn and run but found her feet locked to the floor. Great, a monster dust bunny was headed her way and she had stepped in a sticky old curse some slob had dropped on the floor. She couldn't run now if she wanted to.

Above her, Digby watched. "Yes, you can, ReeCee. Today IS that day," he whispered.

Edweena rushed by and shoved her, screaming, "Beau, Beau, help me! Save me, Beau!"

Behind Digby, Beau whimpered and buried his head under his clothes.

ReeCee racked her brain to remember a curse, spell, hex,

anything, but it all jumbled together. The dust bunny was so close now that she could see Mrs. Snaglkrum rolling around in its great fuzzly innards. Digby was right, it did look hungry.

Racing along behind the dust bunny were Principal Haydeez, teachers, and the skeletons. Principal Haydeez and the teachers were brandishing wands, while the skeletons were waving brooms and wastebaskets.

As ReeCee stared at the oncoming humungous glob of dust, fuzzels, and air, she suddenly realized that it wasn't one single dust bunny. It was actually hundreds of them all stuck together just like the ones she had given to Oliver.

Oliver! This was his project!

Wait . . . Digby was right! She did know what to do. She pointed her finger. "One by one you came, and one by one you'll go. Here and now, right out that door." She swung her finger from the monstrous dust bunny to the door.

Small, individual dust bunnies began to fly off. They hit the floor and started frantically rolling around, trying to find their way out the door. The skeletons chased after them with their brooms and wastebaskets.

As they began to pile up against the front doors, Principal Haydeez quickly tapped his wand against the carved wood, entering the code that would undo the seal holding the doors closed. As the doors began to swing open, the dust bunnies scurried out. They tumbled wildly down the steps and scattered as soon as they hit the sidewalk.

In a few minutes, only a couple of dust bunnies were left struggling to get out of Mrs. Snaglkrum's hair. Principal Haydeez helped Mrs. Snalgkrum to her feet, and one of the other teachers freed the little creatures. In a moment, they, too, were out the door.

As the last of them vanished into the night, Principal Haydeez closed and resealed the door.

Principal Haydeez looked down at ReeCee. "You are a very brave young witch. Your magic did what no one else's could. Thank you."

The chimes in the clock tower began their sepulcher tones. It was exactly midnight.

The skeletons looked at each other and at the cleaning equipment in their bony hands. They tossed everything aside and headed back to the gym with Mrs. Snaglkrum right behind them yelling, "Hold on, I haven't finished determining who cast the spell on you!"

Principal Haydeez flicked his wand, activating the intercauldron system. "Now that the excitement is over and you will all live to start another school week, may I suggest that everyone get back to the gym. It's time for the trick or treat drop."

As quickly as they had poured into the great hall, students raced back to the gym where the noise approached a level that would soon crack the school's old stones. Principal Haydeez disappeared as well.

Digby came down the stairs, followed by Beau. Stopping, Beau looked around carefully to assure himself that no one else was around. "I just wanna say thanks. It would have been pretty uncool for everybody to find out puberty is just not happening for me yet. You won't tell Dalen or anyone else, will you?" he asked anxiously.

Digby put his hand on Beau's shoulder. "Our lips are sealed. Promise."

Beau ducked his head in thanks. "Look guys, it's not that I want to be ungrateful about tonight, but when you're in junior high, it's just not cool to talk to lower life forms in front of your friends."

"That's okay," Digby said. "We're not really into talking to alien life forms anyway, so we're good."

Beau grinned and knuckle-bumped Digby before heading toward the gym.

Digby turned back to ReeCee. "Wanna go see if there are any treats left?"

"Yeah, I guess so." ReeCee sounded oddly dispirited.

"Okay, you just did the best magic of your life and saved everyone from being sucked into a giant dust bunny. What's the problem?"

"Digby, I'm the worst witch in Williwog Woods! Nothing I do ever comes out right. Maybe it wasn't me that did it. Maybe Oliver's project was going to fall apart anyway."

"No, ReeCee, it was your magic that stopped the dust bunny," Principal Haydeez said, popping out of a cloud of smoke. "You have a very ancient and powerful magic. It comes directly from your heart. When you cast, your magic will always create the right outcome, which may not be the intended outcome. That's why once your spell is done, it can't be undone. No one in Williwog Woods has the ability to undo 'right' magic."

She thought about that for a moment and then asked "Does that mean I'm still gonna mess up my spells?"

"Yup. But I'll take a gumdrop over a fly any day." He squatted down. "ReeCee, you still have to grow into your magic, but when you do, you will be one amazing witch."

"A real witch?"

"The realest witch these old Woods have seen in centuries. Now, you two, I think if you look behind the tombstone in the farthest corner of the graveyard, you just might find a couple of bags of treats."

ReeCee and Digby looked at each other. "First one there," Digby said.

ReeCee stood still for a moment as an understanding settled into her heart. She wasn't ever going to be the witch others expected. Instead, she was going to be exactly the witch SHE was supposed to be, and that was okay. Maybe even better than okay.

Then, with a whoop, the very real witch-in-the-making took off running.

Author Bio

L. Lee Shaw is the owner of the Indie publishing house, Boho Books. In 2017, she debuted the award-winning young adult novel, *Aging Out*. She has previously published the YA *Monster Child* and several books for grown-ups.

Learn more at www.bohobooks.com

Illustrator Bio

Linda Brewster has received numerous awards for her paintings and photographs in Philadelphia, PA. She has also received awards for her book, *Rose O'Neill: The Girl Who Loved to Draw.*

Learn More at http://www.lindabrewster.com

CPSIA information can be obtained
at www.ICGtesting.com
Printed in the USA
BVHW07s1638040918
526483BV00003B/19/P

9 780990 707301